DISNEY
fairies

Myka
Finds
Her
Way

Myka Finds Her Way

WRITTEN BY
GAIL HERMAN

ILLUSTRATED BY
DENISE SHIMABUKURO,
DEE FARNSWORTH & CONSTANCE ALLEN

RANDOM HOUSE  NEW YORK

Library of Congress Cataloging-in-Publication Data

Herman, Gail.

Myka finds her way / written by Gail Herman ; illustrated by Denise
Shimabukuro, Dee Farnsworth & Constance Allen.

p.   cm.

Summary: As a sharp-eyed fairy scout in Pixie Hollow,
Myka protects the other fairies from dangers, but after her eyesight
begins to worsen, she uses her other senses to convince everyone that
she still can see and do her job.

ISBN 978-0-7364-2606-0 (pbk.)

[1. Fairies—Fiction. 2. Vision—Fiction. 3. Senses and sensation—Fiction.]
I. Shimabukuro, Denise, ill. II. Farnsworth, Dee, ill.
III. Allen, Constance, ill. IV. Title.

PZ7.H4315Mym 2010

[E]—dc22   2008054576

www.randomhouse.com/kids

Printed in the United States of America

10 9 8 7 6 5 4 3 2 1

All About Fairies

IF YOU HEAD toward the second star on your right and fly straight on till morning, you'll come to Never Land, a magical island where mermaids play and children never grow up.

When you arrive, you might hear something like the tinkling of little bells. Follow that sound and you'll find Pixie Hollow, the secret heart of Never Land.

A great old maple tree grows in Pixie Hollow, and in it live hundreds of fairies and sparrow men. Some of them can do water magic, others can fly like the wind, and still others can speak to animals. You see, Pixie Hollow is the Never fairies' kingdom, and each fairy who lives there has a special, extraordinary talent.

Not far from the Home Tree, nestled in the branches of a hawthorn, is Mother Dove, the most magical creature of all. She sits on her egg, watching over the fairies, who in turn watch over her. For as long as Mother Dove's egg stays well and whole, no one in Never Land will ever grow old.

Once, Mother Dove's egg *was* broken. But we are not telling the story of the egg here. Now it is time for Myka's tale. . . .

Myka
Finds
Her
Way

1

MYKA WOKE WITH a start. She leaped from her bed and landed lightly on her toes. Some sort of noise had just echoed through Pixie Hollow. It could mean trouble. Fully alert, she darted to her bedroom window.

Myka's room was in the uppermost branch of the Home Tree. A knothole window stretched from floor to ceiling along an entire wall.

Myka slipped her sea-glass binoculars from the peg by her bed. Then she gazed out the window. Not one leaf rustled. Not one moth beat its wings.

But while she'd been sleeping, she *had* heard a noise. She was certain of it. The noise had made her toes tingle. But now . . . now . . . the air was still. In the darkness before sunrise, even the birds and crickets were silent.

Yet her instincts told her something was wrong.

Myka was a scouting-talent fairy. Her job was to warn other fairies of danger. She kept on guard for hawks and owls and other animals that preyed on fairies. She sniffed for out-of-control fires on the far side of Never Land. And she listened for angry wasps buzzing near Havendish Stream. All five of Myka's senses were razor-sharp.

And if a noise woke her in the middle of the night, she was ready to check it out. It was all part of being a scout.

Myka couldn't waste another minute. She reached for her quiver, which was filled with porcupine quill darts. Then she flew outside.

Darkness pressed in close. Myka felt as if she were the only fairy in the world. She circled the Home Tree. Nothing. She flew through Pixie Hollow. For a wingbeat, she hovered over a patch of itchy ivy. Then she flew on.

Suddenly, she heard the noise. *Boom!* There was a low rumble in the distance. A flash lit the sky.

Myka had to get closer. She had to see what was happening. She flew toward the noise and lights. The rumblings turned to roars. The flashes grew brighter.

Everything looked strange in the on-again, off-again flare of light. *Boom!*

She saw a gnarled tree bent over, its bare branches sweeping the ground. *Boom!* She spotted a towering beehive. It swayed from the thick trunk of a maple tree.

She swerved around it and kept flying. *Boom!* The spooky light cast long shadows from trees . . . plants . . . rocks.

Everything seemed different. But she was a scout. She had to keep going.

Besides, she was curious about what was going on. The sky was growing brighter now. Spying an open field, Myka settled to the ground.

Round red flowers covered the field. Their petals gathered together at the tips.

Why, she thought, *they look like fluffy balls. I wonder if Lily would know what they are.*

Poof! Each flower let out a puff of tangy air. Myka waved a hand to clear it away from her face. All her senses tingled. Something was about to happen. She forgot about the strange flowers.

A dark shape moved across the sky. Was it a giant black cloud?

Bang! Crash! An ear-splitting roar shook the field. The sky lit up with a dazzling brightness. Lightning! Myka realized. And thunder!

A major storm was brewing. And the way the wind was blowing, it would hit the Home Tree in no time.

Myka took off for Pixie Hollow.

Now she didn't stop to wonder about the sights and sounds. She flew with all her strength.

Home at last! She zipped through her open window. Already she was sounding the alarm. She blew three sharp blasts on a reed whistle by her bed. Danger! Danger! Danger! She flew through the halls, pounding on doors.

"Wake up!" she shouted.

Sleepy fairies poked their heads out of their rooms.

Bess, an art talent, wrapped her smocklike robe around her. "What is it?"

"Thunderstorm!" Myka called over her shoulder. "A big one! Check for weak branches! Latch your windows!"

Other scouts were already moving—

helping and guiding fairies and sparrow men.

"Our rooms are all set!" said Beck. She drew the other animal talents to her side. "Now what should we do?"

"We'll have to wait it out!" Myka prodded a slow-moving Tinker Bell. "Everyone! To the root cellar. We'll be safe there. Come on, come on!"

She herded fairies down through the trunk of the Home Tree. "Hurry! Over here!" She pointed into the dark, windowless space by the roots.

"There," Myka said, finally satisfied. The fairies sat huddled together in row upon row. They were all fully awake. And most looked scared. "The only thing we can do is wait."

So the fairies waited. Time passed, and they waited some more. Some fairies slumped against the bumpy walls and fell asleep again. A few talked quietly.

Myka paced back and forth. She kept one ear cocked, listening. Finally, a rumbling noise made everyone sit up straight.

"Oops!" Tink rubbed her stomach. "Just feeling a little hungry, I guess."

Myka nodded. "We all are," she said. "But we shouldn't go anywhere. The storm will be here any second."

Bess edged closer to Myka. Her face was pale. "You know," she said, "Vidia is still out there."

Vidia, a fast-flying fairy, lived by herself in a sour-plum tree. She liked it

that way. And Myka had to admit, the other fairies did, too. Vidia could be sly—a little nasty, in fact. Still, Vidia shouldn't be out there alone. Not with a dangerous thunderstorm on the way.

The news spread from fairy to sparrow man to fairy. "Vidia is outside!" "Vidia is in trouble!"

Everyone turned to Myka.

"I'll go warn her!" Myka leaped through the door.

"Hooray for Myka!" shouted Tink.

Another scout talent, Trak, followed more slowly behind. "Wait, Myka!" he called. "I'll come, too."

But Myka didn't hear him. She was so determined to find Vidia, she didn't notice Trak—or anything else.

"Vidia!" she cried. "Vidia! There's a thunderstorm! Stay calm! I'm coming!"

Kicking up a puff of dirt, Myka landed by Vidia's sour-plum tree. She looked around, hands on hips. "Well," she said, surprised. "What do you know!"

The sky was a dazzling blue. The sun shone brightly. There was no storm in sight.

And Vidia sat calmly on a branch outside her home.

"Why, what's wrong, Myka?" Vidia asked in her fake-sweet voice. "You didn't think there was any danger, did you?" She shook her head, as if in pity for the poor mistaken scout.

Myka didn't say anything. Of

course she had thought there was danger!

What was going on?

Vidia pointed toward the lagoon. Captain Hook's pirate ship bobbed in the water. "It's just some cannon practice, darling," she said. "They're about ready to fire again."

Boom! Crash! An ear-splitting noise filled the air. Sparks flew. Lights flashed as the cannon flared.

It *had* been the pirates—not thunder and lightning. Black smoke rose like a giant storm cloud from the ship.

Vidia was right. There'd been no danger. No danger at all.

2

MYKA'S FIRST THOUGHT was to alert the others. She had to tell everyone it was safe to come out of hiding. She whirled around.

Bump! She crashed into Trak, who had just caught up.

Trak gave the clear sky a puzzled look. And in truth, Myka was a little puzzled, too. She'd never made such a big mistake before. Not even right after she had arrived.

Myka thought back to her very first day in Never Land. She'd landed on the topmost branch of a towering eucalyptus tree. Pixie Hollow was spread out below.

Dozens of fairies and sparrow men had hovered in the air. They had peered at Myka anxiously. When would she make her Announcement? Which talent group would she join?

Right away, Myka's eyes had settled on one sparrow man, Trak. His dark green clothes blended in with the leaves. But when he fluttered up to the sky, they turned a light blue. Camouflage, Myka now knew. It hid the scout from predators while he watched over Pixie Hollow.

Myka's own Arrival Garment had changed color to match the eucalyptus. "I am a scout!" she'd said loudly.

Trak had cheered. Later, he had helped her build her first lookout—right in that same eucalyptus. He had shown her how to make darts out of quills, and binoculars out of sea glass. He'd answered her questions and given her tours of Never Land. And when she had proved to be the most gifted of all the scouts, he'd patted her on the back and said, "Good job!"

Now Myka waved for Trak to follow her back to the root cellar.

"I was wrong," Myka said. She wasn't

about to make excuses. "There isn't any thunderstorm."

"What?" Trak said. "You made a mistake?"

Myka shrugged. It was a little embarrassing, sure. But what would have happened if she hadn't woken everyone up and there'd really been danger? That would have been much worse.

"Yes, I made a mistake," she said.

A few minutes later, she repeated that to all the fairies and sparrow men in the root cellar. "I'd fly backward if I could," she apologized. She spoke in a strong voice. She looked at as many fairies as possible. For a long moment, she held Queen Clarion's gaze.

"It was the pirates," Myka explained.

"They were firing their ship's cannon."

Everyone stared at her, stunned into silence.

Finally, Dulcie stood and dusted herself off. "Well, I guess I can start breakfast, then. Pecan waffles, anyone?"

Fairies murmured, stood up, and stretched. One by one, they filed past Myka on their way out. She nodded at each one. She hoped they understood. She'd never made a big mistake before. And she wouldn't make another one.

Bess patted her gently on the shoulder. "These things happen," she told her friend. "Once, I mixed colors to paint a sunrise and got a dull shade of brown."

Myka smiled a little uncomfortably. She knew that Bess wanted to make her feel better. But there was a difference between saving lives and painting pictures. That was why she was a scout. She wanted to make a difference. She wanted to protect Never Land. So she was always on alert. All day, every day.

Even, Myka thought, *when I'm eating Dulcie's pecan waffles.*

Myka flew behind the others to the tearoom. With each flutter of her wings, she felt better.

The whole thing lasted only a few hours, she thought. *It didn't amount to much.*

Sure, fairies liked to gossip. They'd be talking and whispering and chattering about "Myka's Big Mistake."

But soon another fairy would make a

mistake. A water talent might flood the kitchen. A laundry talent might shrink the clothes. Then everyone would forget about her little slipup.

Everyone, she thought, heading for the scouting-talent table, *except Trak and the other scouts.*

The scouts stopped talking as she sat

down. Myka had to say something. Something to lighten the mood.

"Good morning," she said, as if she hadn't just spent hours with them in the root cellar. "How is everyone this fine sunny day?"

Sera laughed. "You know how we are. Tired."

Myka turned to Trak. She hated to disappoint him most of all.

Trak gave an exaggerated yawn. "I'm planning to get extra sleep tonight, Myka . . . unless you're on patrol and sound another warning." Then he winked at her.

Myka grinned. If Trak and the others wanted to tease her, that was perfectly okay. She was the best. And everyone knew it. "I could spy a wasp faster than you, Trak."

A clatter of banging pots came from the kitchen. Myka could hear the baking talents hurrying to make breakfast. Usually, they would have an hour or so to get ready. But with all that time in the root cellar . . .

For a moment, Myka's grin faded. But then Dulcie opened the swinging door to the kitchen and announced, "Breakfast is ready—in record time!"

Serving talents carried in trays of waffles, poppy puff rolls, gooseberry jam, and tea. All around the room, fairies and sparrow men bent their heads toward their plates. They'd been up for hours now, and they were hungry.

Myka reached for a roll. *Breakfast is only a little late*, she thought. *Not a big deal at all.*

After eating, Myka decided to fly to her lookout posts. A while ago, she'd come up with the idea that each corner of Pixie Hollow should have its own special pinecone lookout tower. That way she'd have views in all directions.

Myka used the lookouts every day—sometimes three or four times. Today she started at the eucalyptus tree. Tink needed metal to repair some teapots. So Myka was searching for a copper half-penny. The pirates were always losing them from holes in their pockets.

Scouting duties weren't always about hawks and wasps and snakes. Myka knew that as well as any scout. Sometimes a scout used her talent for something less . . . exciting.

Still, Myka wanted to do a mid-morning patrol. She settled in her tower. She breathed deeply. The leaves smelled like the medicine that Clara, a nursing talent, gave for a cough. But Myka liked it anyway.

She gazed into the distance, at Torth Mountain. All was peaceful.

Turning to face Pixie Hollow, Myka took note of the fairies and sparrow men. They flew here and there, herding butterflies, delivering fairy dust. Bess scurried along, a sheet of leaf paper tucked under her arm. Beck chattered with a chipmunk. All was in order.

Wait a minute! Myka squinted. In a corner of the meadow . . . where caterpillars grazed . . . a strange shape settled close to the ground.

Myka stared harder. The shape shifted. The caterpillars backed away, afraid.

What was it?

Myka flew closer to the field. She hovered in the air. She didn't want to draw attention to herself. Not yet.

The shape was fuzzy, orange, and lumpy. It wriggled this way and that. "Waaah, kew! Waaah, kew!" it moaned. Suddenly, it shuddered. "Waaah, kew!"

What kind of creature was it?

The caterpillars inched away as fast as they could. By now, they were at the edge of the meadow. They hurried to hide in the surrounding trees.

Myka held up her reed whistle, ready to sound an alarm. Then the creature lifted itself off the ground.

"Oh, hi, Myka."

The strange beast knew her name! And the voice sounded familiar. It sounded almost like . . .

The creature threw off its orange covering.

"Nettle!" Myka cried. "It's you!"

"You couldn't tell?" Nettle, who was a caterpillar-shearing talent, yawned. "I was just herding the caterpillars along." She carefully folded the fuzzy blanket.

"You know," she told Myka, "this blanket was woven from the softest hairs of woolly-bear caterpillars."

At the sound of "woolly-bear," the caterpillars—woolly-bear ones, Myka realized—scuttled more quickly.

"They don't like it when I clip their fuzz," Nettle confided to Myka. "They try to run away." She yawned again. "Shearing is hard work."

Myka laughed. "You weren't working very hard just now."

"Well, I have to gather my strength." Nettle's eyes narrowed. "Were you scouting around, checking on me? Did that new shearer put you up to it?"

"Of course not!" Myka protested. Spying on other fairies? No self-respecting scout would ever do that! Sometimes, though, it was bound to happen by accident. Once, she'd discovered two harvest talents, Pluck and Pell, hiding under a weeping willow tree. They were eating the berries they were supposed to be collecting.

Back then, she'd known right away it was Pluck and Pell. She didn't think they were a two-headed berry-eating monster. This time, though, she'd had no clue the mysterious creature was only Nettle.

For the rest of the day, Myka searched for Tink's half-penny and patrolled Pixie Hollow. She didn't see anything unusual. And she didn't find a single coin.

Myka always finished assignments.

A fairy would ask her to look for something. And she'd find it. A button, a coin, a certain kind of pebble. Her eyesight was so sharp, she could pick out any object, anytime.

Not today.

But she'd found so many coins in the past. There probably weren't any around right now. That was all. She'd try again later. She'd be sure to find one then.

All in all, Myka thought, flying back to the Home Tree, *Pixie Hollow is calm and quiet. And that's what counts.*

"Hello, Myka!" Lily flew past, holding a bunch of flowers in one hand and a watering can in the other.

"How pretty!" said Myka.

"I'm going to put the flowers in the

courtyard," Lily said, "so everyone can enjoy them."

Fairies and sparrow men were all heading home for the day. The sky filled with fluttering wings and cheerful voices.

"See you in the tearoom," called Bess.

Myka smiled at her friend. She fluttered lower, into the Home Tree courtyard.

Suddenly, she pulled up short.

There, up ahead! In the shadiest corner, a snake slithered around a rock.

Danger! Danger! Myka's senses cried. Fangs! Fierce! Fairy-catching!

"Watch out!" she shouted. "Yellow-bellied whipsnake!"

3

SCREEE! SCREEE! MYKA blew her whistle
to sound the alarm. "Snake!" she cried.

All around the courtyard, fairies
skidded to a stop. A fast-flying fairy
braked so suddenly, she lost control.
She bumped into Lily. Lily dropped the
flowers and the watering can, spilling
petals and water everywhere.

Fairies and sparrow men panicked.

"What's happening?"

"A snake is in the courtyard!"

They fell into one another, slipping on petals and puddles. They shouted, then flew, then ran, then shouted.

"This way!" Myka tried to herd the fairies out of danger. But no one was listening.

Tweeet! A sharp whistle cut through the noise. Trak hovered over everyone, waving his arms. "Fairies! Sparrow men! It's all right! There is no snake!"

Right away, everyone quieted.

"What?" Myka swung to face him.

"It's only a tree branch," Trak said.

Myka flew to the rock. Trak was right. The soft branch bent around the rock like a coiled snake. Its yellow bark shone in the sunlight.

"No need to panic," Trak went on. "Just go to the tearoom. Dinner is ready."

Trak glanced at Myka, shaking his head. Her glow flared bright pink.

"Well, well," Iris said under her breath as she passed Myka. "That was a lot of excitement . . . for no reason."

Usually, no one paid attention to Iris. She was a garden talent who didn't even have a garden. She just had a plant book filled with little-known facts about flowers and plants. But now, the fairies around her nodded in agreement.

"I'm still tired from this morning," a dusting-talent fairy said pointedly.

The fairies fluttered past Myka.

Some whispered. Some cast sideways looks at her. She heard phrases like "Scouting problem. Don't you think? False alarms. Two of them."

Nettle passed and gave Myka a funny look.

Myka groaned. *Make that* three *false alarms,* she thought.

Then Tink said, "It's okay about the coin, Myka. I don't really need one."

And now Tink didn't think she could find a silly half-penny!

Myka slipped into the shadows. Part of her wanted to disappear. But another, stronger part decided to face everyone. She stood up straight, determined to stay calm and in control. Wasn't that part of being a scouting talent, too?

Trak flew to her side. "What's the matter?" he asked.

"The matter?" Myka repeated. "I made some mistakes. It could happen to any scout."

"Maybe." Trak shot her a look of concern. "Or maybe something is a bit off with your eyesight."

Myka's glow turned pale. "Shhh!" she hissed.

A few fairies still milled around. Had anyone heard? Did anyone else think that, too?

Myka squared her shoulders. So what if they *had* heard? She was still an expert scout. "That's just crazy, Trak," she said. "Nothing's changed."

Trak raised his eyebrows. "If you say

so. I just thought I'd ask." Then he flew into the Home Tree without a second glance.

"Well! Let that old scout think what he wants." Myka humphed. "It doesn't bother me." She almost convinced herself that it was true.

Bess touched her arm. "Are you okay, Myka?" she asked.

Myka blurted, "Trak thinks something's wrong with my eyes. Imagine! Telling a scout something like that! It's like . . . it's like . . . telling an art talent she can't paint! You just can't say that!"

"So what do you think?" Bess asked.

The truth was, Myka didn't know what to think. Was her eyesight failing? Or, as she'd told Trak, had she just made mistakes? Very big, very embarrassing mistakes?

Myka sighed, annoyed. Either way, she'd lost everyone's trust. And without trust, how could a scout keep scouting?

Myka had to prove herself—just like a newly arrived fairy.

Myka paced back and forth in her room. Her pussy-willow moccasins barely made a sound against the floor.

"Okay," she said. "I have to prove myself to everyone. I just have to be the first scout to spot the next danger."

Of course, Myka didn't want anything horrible to happen. But maybe a small hawk could circle the Home Tree.

Then she could step in. She'd warn the others and help the animal talents come up with a plan.

"I'd save the day!" she whispered.

But if there weren't any hawks around? What then? It could be a wasp. Or anything, really. She just had to spot some kind of trouble.

In all of Never Land, there had to be something happening. Right now.

Myka jumped into the air. She'd fly to her lookout at the eucalyptus tree. The sun was going to set soon. Already, the light was dim. But surely she had enough time.

Without wasting another moment, Myka darted outside. She flew quickly, feeling confident. That corner of Pixie

Hollow was always chillier than the other three. The wind blew more strongly there. Myka felt the breeze whip her hair. She'd be at the lookout any second!

Wait a minute. . . . There was Havendish Stream. And she was flying over a thick forest. In her haste, she'd flown right past the eucalyptus. That had never happened before!

Chuckling a little nervously, Myka wheeled around. A vine brushed her cheek, startling her. She gulped.

Everything looked so dim. She couldn't tell the shapes from the shadows. The wind gusted. Branches swayed. She could barely see a thing!

But the breeze carried a scent—that medicine-y smell of eucalyptus leaves. She sniffed. Over there! It was coming from that direction!

The scent grew stronger as Myka neared the tree. At last, she settled on a leaf. Now all she had to do was fly to the top and find the lookout!

Staying close to the trunk, Myka

made her way up. A dark shape loomed in front of her. The lookout! Panting, she scrambled onto the platform. She leaned back to rest. Bit by bit, her breathing slowed.

Whew! Myka had to laugh. What kind of scout couldn't find her own lookout?

"A tired scout," Myka told herself. And now that she thought about it, she really was worn out. Her eyes felt gritty. She could barely see the tree twenty wing-flaps away.

Why had she been in such a hurry? Tomorrow was another day. She'd head back to the Home Tree now. Get a good night's sleep. She'd find danger in the morning, when it wasn't so dark.

4

THE NEXT DAY, Myka woke at dawn, as usual. Right away, she knew she wouldn't be scouting. Her eyesight hadn't gotten better, not one bit. If anything, objects looked dimmer. The sunlight seemed less bright.

"It's not a big deal," Myka told herself. So she wouldn't go out on patrol—at least not today. There were plenty of other ways to be a scout. Plenty of ways to convince everyone she could be trusted. She'd just have to start smaller.

And she knew right where to begin.

Myka flew down the Home Tree hallway. She poked her head into the sewing room. "Anyone here?" she called out. Already, sewing talents were working busily. They sat in a circle, stitching a tablecloth. Scissors snapped. Needles flashed. Fairies chattered.

"I came for a visit!" Myka called more loudly.

Most of the sewing talents didn't look up. Others glanced at each other, but nobody met Myka's eyes.

Myka frowned. This was annoying!

How could she help anyone this way? Well, she'd just have to do her best.

Myka sidled up to Hem. The other fairies shifted away. "That's a lovely cross-stitch," she told Hem.

"Actually, it's a butterfly stitch," Hem corrected her.

Myka cleared her throat. "Well, it's still lovely." Then she raised her voice. "Anyone need some scouting help this morning? Anyone need a new supply of silk thread? Maybe some angora?"

The fairies bent their heads closer to the tablecloth. No one answered.

Myka plowed on. "How about you, Hem?"

Hem shook her head.

"Come on," Myka said in a jolly

voice. "I'm sure you can think of something for me to do."

Hem sighed. "Okay," she said at last. "I lost a needle a few days ago. Right in this room. I searched and I searched, and I can't find it. Can you?"

Now it was Myka's turn to sigh. What a dull task! She didn't even need to leave the room! But it was something to do. And a way to show everyone that she could still scout.

"Sure!" she said loudly, so that everybody could hear. "I'll get right on it!"

Myka fluttered low to the floor—so low, she stubbed her toe. Even there, she couldn't see much of anything.

She sank even lower. She bumped her nose on the ground. "Ouch!" she

whispered. Covering up the pain, she sat down.

"Double ouch!" She'd sat on something sharp. She reached down and pulled out the missing needle.

"Aha!" she cried. She really had gotten right on it!

"I found it!" she called.

"Wow," said Hem. "That was fast!"

"What was fast?" Dulcie flew into the room. She carried a basket of muffins for the sewing talents.

"Myka scouted out a lost needle, quick as a running stitch."

"It was nothing." Myka bowed her head modestly. "It's easy, when you have my sharp eyesight."

"So." Dulcie pulled her aside. "You had a successful search. But what about those false alarms?"

Myka shrugged. "All in the past. I'm in fine form now."

"Good! Just in time to help me!" Dulcie said. "Could you search out some bellflowers? I'd like to use them as dessert dish covers. They're shaped just like bells, I hear."

This was slightly more exciting than looking for a lost needle. At least she'd be out of the Home Tree. Even better, Dulcie trusted her.

"It's for my four-layer maple cake," Dulcie added.

Myka's favorite!

Myka rushed to Lily's garden. Bess was sitting in one corner, sketching a clump of violets. Iris was next to her. "The petals should be more *round*," she advised. Myka flew over to them.

"Iris," Myka said. "Just the fairy I wanted to see! I need to search out bellflowers for Dulcie. Can you help me?"

"All right," Iris said grudgingly. She opened her plant book. "The bellflower grows in all sorts of places—"

"Here," Bess broke in. "I can copy the picture for you." She began to draw.

Iris went on and on, telling Myka more about the flower than she'd ever need to know. "And finally," she added, out of breath, "there are three hundred different kinds, from blue to purple to white to pink."

"There!" said Bess, finishing her sketch. "All done!"

Myka grabbed the leaf paper. "Thank you . . . both! I'm off!"

Minutes later, she was circling a field on the edge of Pixie Hollow. In one hand she held a balloon carrier to carry the flowers. In the other hand, she held the picture—right under her nose, so she could see it more clearly.

I can do this, Myka thought. *Iris said these flowers grow all over.*

She wrinkled her brow and squinted. No, there weren't any bellflowers in that field. Or in the meadow. But along the banks of a small, clear stream, she found a patch of white and purple flowers. They hung from their stems like perfectly shaped bells.

"Got them!" she cried.

Myka gathered the flowers. Carefully, she placed them in the balloon carrier. Then she flew back to Pixie Hollow, losing her way only once, when she mistook a rock for a bush. At the Home Tree, she unhooked the basket. Then she left it—flowers and all—outside the kitchen.

Dulcie peeked out. "Just right!" she said. She brought in the basket, leaving Myka alone.

Suddenly, a wave of dismay swept over Myka. The thrill of finding the flowers and making her way home had worn off. Now she had to admit the truth. After searching so long and so hard, she knew for sure.

"Something is definitely wrong with my eyes," she said out loud.

Myka quickly looked around. No one was there. Good. It was one thing to admit it to herself. It was quite another for someone else to hear.

5

"There you are, Myka."

Myka was still standing outside the kitchen window, thinking. She heard Trak's voice and looked up.

"I hear you found a missing needle." He glanced into the kitchen. "And also those dessert covers for Dulcie?"

Myka nodded.

"Well, then. Ahem." He coughed. "I guess I was wrong about your eyes."

Myka squinted at Trak. His edges were blurry, and she couldn't see his face very well.

"How about we do some group patrols?" Sera suggested, joining them.

A group patrol? Myka couldn't do that! The other scouts would surely realize she couldn't see.

"I'd love to," Myka said in a rush. "But I have to, ah . . . ah . . . I told Bess I'd look for a landscape for her to paint."

Before her friends could say a word, Myka darted inside. She passed Tink's workshop. Tink waved from the door. At least, Myka thought she waved. Really, she wasn't even sure it was Tink.

Myka pressed close to the Home Tree walls. She hid behind the tall plants in the corners. She didn't want anyone to see her . . . or where she was going.

Myka paused in the hall. She looked left and right. All clear. Quickly, she opened a door and slipped through. The sign by the door read *Infirmary*.

Inside, a nursing talent placed twig-splints in neat piles.

Myka took two steps toward her. "Oof!" She tripped over a stool.

I didn't even see that! she thought.

"Myka?" The nursing talent hurried over.

"Oh, Clara. It's you." Myka recognized the voice. She heard Clara setting the stool upright.

"Now, what brings you here?" Clara spoke in a brisk, no-nonsense voice.

"You haven't heard?" Myka asked hopefully. "About me having any sort of problem?"

Clara busied herself with a birch-bark clipboard. She flipped over a sheet of leaf paper.

Myka had never been to the infirmary before—she'd never had any reason to visit. But she knew that each fairy had her own clipboard, filled with information. Her Arrival Day. Her talent. Her hair and eye color. Where she lived in the Home Tree.

Finally, Clara spoke. "Oh, Myka, nursing talents don't listen to gossip. We examine each fairy with an open mind. It

doesn't help to think we know the problem before we do a checkup." She pointed to a sign written in Leaf Letters.

Myka could barely see the letters. But at least she could tell that the sign was in the ancient writing. "I can't read old Leaf Lettering," she said honestly.

"'First, keep an open mind,'" Clara

said. "It's our nursing-talent motto."

Clara washed her hands with a piece of soapstone. "Now, let me check your eyes."

Myka grinned. She almost said, "How do you know something is wrong with my eyes? Have you been listening to gossip?" Instead, she sat on the stool and opened her eyes wide.

Clara's glow flared as she peered first at Myka's left eye, then her right.

"Hmm," Clara said. She scribbled on her clipboard. "Now, when did this trouble start?"

Myka thought back. "I guess the other morning. When I thought there was a thunderstorm? I scouted all over Never Land."

"Where exactly did you fly?" Clara asked.

As best she could, Myka went back through her flight. Pixie Hollow. The forest. The meadow. The field. The lagoon. Clara nodded along.

"Can you read this eye chart?" The nursing talent pulled down a rolled-up leaf paper hanging high on the wall.

Myka shook her head. She could barely see the chart!

Clara put down the clipboard. "Myka, I'd say you're having a vision problem."

Myka gritted her teeth. Any fairy could have told her that! Still, she said nothing.

"But I'm not sure why. You've been

working hard. You might have just strained your eyes," Clara said.

"What does it mean?" Myka was growing impatient. "What can I do?"

"Nothing much." Clara wrote a note on Myka's clipboard. "Just rest your eyes. They should heal by themselves." She handed Myka a pile of mosscloths. "Cover your eyes with these."

Good news, bad news, Myka thought. Good news, she'd be better in no time! Bad news, she had to rest her eyes. A scout couldn't really do that!

"Listen, Clara." Myka spoke in a low voice. "Could you keep quiet about all this? I really don't want this sort of thing to get around Pixie Hollow."

"Of course I'll keep it quiet." Clara

pointed to another sign in Leaf Letters. "We take a privacy pledge. Anything that happens between a patient and a nursing talent is strictly hush-hush."

Myka was a patient? She'd never been sick a day in her life! But if it would keep Clara quiet, then she guessed it was fine.

Myka went to her room. She covered her eyes with cool mosscloths. And she waited, tapping her toes impatiently on her bed's footboard.

Hours passed. Finally, she heard the flurry of wings in the halls. It was time for dinner.

Okay, she thought. *All I have to do is take off this mosscloth and I'll be perfectly fine. I can get back to work.*

Smiling happily, she removed the mosscloth. "Oh, no!" She drew in her breath. Her eyesight was even worse!

Her nightstand looked like a shapeless blob. Her bed was a bigger blob.

Oh, tracks and trails! She couldn't bear to stay in her room, resting, another minute! She had to move, had to track, had to scout.

Would it make that much difference if she got up and got going? Clara had said her eyes would heal by themselves, hadn't she? And didn't that mean with or without rest?

Myka felt around under the bed. She pulled out her shoes, then slipped them on. Somehow, she'd have to act the way she always did. Somehow, she'd disguise the fact that she even had a problem.

Myka stood up tall. She was ready . . . for dinner.

She flew down the hallway but paused at the door to the tearoom. Getting there was simple. She'd flown up and down the Home Tree halls so often, she could do it in her sleep. She knew the layout of the tearoom as well. The scout table stood along the far end, facing the biggest window. All the scouts sat there in a row, looking out into Pixie Hollow.

Myka stepped lightly into the room. It should be fine if no one flew too close. . . .

"Watch out, Myka!" A fast-flying fairy zipped past. Myka pressed herself against the wall. She waited a moment. But she couldn't just stand there forever. Was anyone else coming?

Her nose and ears tingled, and her fingertips itched. Her other senses were on high alert.

Myka heard the kitchen door swing open. From inside came the soft clatter of plates being lifted off trays. The aroma of sweet biscuits drifted past.

A fairy fluttered close by. She smelled of flour and cocoa and cinnamon.

Dulcie!

"Dinner looks delicious, Dulcie," Myka said.

"We're having my four-layer maple cake tonight!" Dulcie told her. "Thanks to your help, of course! I'll ask the serving talents to serve the scout table first, in your honor."

Myka sniffed. Was that a lavender scent now? "Why, Lily!" she cried. "Late for dinner?"

"Just a little!" Lily laughed. "You're not even sitting yet!"

Smiling and nodding at fairies she could barely see, Myka made her way to the scout table. She strained to hear every voice.

"Look, there's Myka."

"She actually found a needle, and the dish covers for Dulcie!"

"I guess she doesn't have a problem after all."

"Did you see the new portrait of Queen Clarion?"

"I did! It looks absolutely lovely!"

"I passed it in the lobby just now!"

Myka edged around some chairs. Now she smelled berry paint and brush cleaner.

"Congratulations, Bess!" she said to the dim shape in front of her. "Your portrait is a big success!"

"That's nice of you to say, Myka," Bess replied.

It's working! Myka thought. *I have everyone fooled!*

She slipped into her usual seat at the scout table. She nodded all around, hoping she was actually looking at fairies.

She worked extra hard at reaching for dishes. She couldn't see much. But she sensed objects, and that was a help.

Serving talents whisked away plates. Myka sighed. Dinner was almost over. Only dessert remained.

"So." She turned to Trak, sitting on her right. "Should we plan that group patrol?"

"Sounds good," Trak began. He paused so that a serving talent could place dessert on the table. "Let's—"

"Stop, everyone! Stop!" Iris rushed into the tearoom. Myka had no trouble recognizing her panicked voice. "Don't eat the cake! Don't even touch it!" she shrieked.

"Why, what's the matter?" Dulcie hurried in after her.

Iris whirled to face her. "Those dessert dish covers Myka brought you?

They're not bellflowers. They're phlox-gloves!" She waved her book in the air as proof.

Myka's heart sank. Did that make a difference?

"Phloxgloves are poisonous!" Iris cried. "The cake is poisoned!"

Everyone gasped, then fell silent. Myka felt their stares. Quickly, she stood up. Her chair fell backward.

No one else moved.

Myka edged clumsily from the table. Flustered and upset, she couldn't find her way.

She smelled berry paint and knew Bess was at her side. "It's all right," Bess said. "No one was hurt. Don't worry."

"Yes, Myka. Don't worry." Myka

heard Queen Clarion's calm, steady voice from across the room. She felt the air move around her, and the queen stood next to her. "The kitchen and cleaning talents will scrub everything free of poison—including themselves."

Myka took a deep breath, relieved. Then she felt everyone's eyes still on her. They were all judging the scout who couldn't tell one flower from another.

They all knew her eyesight was failing.

Queen Clarion touched her arm. "But Myka, I need to see you in my chambers."

6

Queen Clarion led Myka to her sitting room. "I've asked Clara to come, too," the queen explained. "I thought it might be helpful."

The queen was being kind. But Myka knew what she really meant. The nursing talent would make sure she didn't try to scout—maybe ever again.

Just at that moment, Clara flew in. Myka heard the sound of her wings.

"Now then." Queen Clarion settled onto the couch. Myka and Clara sat on chairs across from her. "It seems to me that Myka should be off duty."

"But—" Myka interrupted.

The queen held up a hand. "For now, just for now." Her voice was calm and soothing. "This isn't a punishment. No one doubts how much you want to help. But this is for your own good. You need time to heal."

"That's just what I told her!" Clara put in.

"I know you're not happy about this," the queen went on. "But you have to wear the mosscloth all day, every day."

Clara scribbled on her clipboard.

"B-b-but then I won't be able to see at all!" Myka protested. "How can I do—"

"Exactly!" said the queen with a smile. "You can't do anything—but rest."

Clara wrapped the moss around Myka's eyes. Everything went dark. This was so unfair! Doing this to a scouting talent!

Myka sniffed. Berry paint!

Bess must have come in. "Bess will take you to your room now," Queen Clarion said. "I hope you feel better."

Myka nodded, miserable. Her room! She'd be stuck there. Just like a bird with a broken wing, unable to leave her nest.

"You'll see," Bess said as she guided Myka through the halls. "You'll be better in no time."

She patted Myka on the shoulder. "We're here. Will you be okay in your bedroom?" Bess asked.

There was no way Myka was going to stay inside. A prisoner!

"Sure," said Myka. "Fly with you later."

She waited for Bess to turn and go. Then, trailing behind, she followed Bess's scent—all through the Home Tree and outside to her studio.

"Myka!" Bess spun toward her, surprised.

"See?" Myka grumbled. "I can still get around. I'm not totally useless."

"No one said you were. But what about resting?" Bess asked.

"I can rest right here," Myka said.

"I guess so. It would probably be lonely up there, anyway," Bess agreed. "But you still need to keep that moss on!"

Myka smiled. At least she'd scored one small victory. "Need any scouting work done?"

Bess led her to a small walnut table. Myka began pulling mouse hairs from a pile. Using her sense of touch, she could find the very finest hairs. Bess would want those for her new paintbrush.

"Everything started when I landed in that field of strange flowers." Myka shook her head in disgust.

"Strange? How?" Bess asked.

"Well, the flower petals came together in a ball shape. Then they opened up and puffed air." Myka thought for a moment. "Those bursts of air were so sharp and strong. I can almost smell them now!"

Bess was quiet for a moment. "Hmm. I feel like I've seen those flowers somewhere. . . . They puffed air. . . ."

Suddenly, Bess jumped up. "Come with me!" She took Myka by the elbow and led her back to the Home Tree, through the hall, and to an out-of-the-way branch. In the back, near the top, Myka guessed. She'd never even known there were rooms here.

Bess pushed open the chipped, heavy door. "Not many fairies know about this room," she explained. "Really, only art talents."

Myka stood at the door. Then she edged inside, feeling around. "Careful!" Bess warned.

Myka's fingers told her that cracked

and peeling paintings lined the walls. In one corner, she felt pictures stacked floor to ceiling. In another corner, dusty books filled a honeycomb bookcase.

"What is this place?"

"It's not quite a storage room and not quite a museum," Bess explained. "It's a little of both. This is where we keep all the ancient paintings. Some are very powerful, like this painting of Havendish Stream on a foggy morning."

Bess pulled Myka close to one painting. Myka felt mist swirling from the picture, settling around her.

Bess, meanwhile, was lifting paintings and searching in corners. "I seem to remember one picture in particular. It reminds me of that field."

Carefully, Bess moved some paintings out of the way. "Here it is!"

Myka heard her grunt, then carry a painting closer. Oh, how she wished she could see! Myka touched the canvas. It felt flower-petal soft. Then she smelled it. Nothing.

She heard a low hiss. Then she smelled again. And there it was—that same tangy scent!

"That's it, Bess," Myka said. "Those are the flowers. I remember the smell!"

"Myka, I just remembered a story about the art talent who made this painting. It's a pepper puff field. And while he was painting it, his eyesight started going. He could hardly see at all."

Bess grabbed Myka's hand. "Maybe

that's what's happening!" she said. "You landed in the pepper puffs. And the spray from the flowers is hurting your eyesight!"

Myka took another sniff. The plants in the painting were the same plants she had seen in the field. She felt sure of it.

"Let's tell Clara," Bess said. "Now that we know what caused it—"

"She may know how to fix it!" Myka cut in. She let Bess lead her out of the room and straight to the infirmary.

7

Clara opened a tattered book and flipped through its pages.

"This is the tale of the pepper puff plant," she explained. "According to legend, the plant has a powerful, dangerous spray. If a fairy lands in a pepper field early in the morning, the flowers wake up cranky and out of sorts. They let out bursts of peppery spray. If the spray settles on a fairy, it weakens her eyesight."

"So?" Bess asked eagerly. "What else does the book say? Is there a cure?"

Clara frowned and shook her head.

"What?" Myka leaned forward. "Did I miss something?"

She'd been letting Bess do the talking. But she was curious about the legend.

"The only tried and tested cure is rest," Clara told them.

Disappointed, Myka turned to leave.

"Wait," said Clara slowly.

Beside Myka, Bess's wings fluttered with excitement. "Go on, Clara. Please!"

"Well," Clara continued, "the book

does mention a very ancient story of another cure. But it's never been proved. A bandage made from shimmer moss. The moss grows in one place in Never Land and one place only—a cave behind Indigo Falls."

"Indigo Falls?" Myka repeated. "That huge waterfall in Tammarin Gorge? I never knew there was a cave there."

"Well, there's a reason you didn't know about it. It's kept secret."

"Why?" Myka asked.

"The cave is filled with danger. The bewitched water of the falls snuffs out fairy glows. Inside, it's darker than any other place."

Myka laughed. Right now her whole world was as black as a starless night. "That would hardly bother me!"

"There's a bottomless pit right in its center," Clara went on.

"So?" Myka shrugged. "I can just fly over it."

"Your wings will be wet from the waterfall. You won't be able to fly."

"Is that all?" asked Myka.

Clara shook her head. "No," she

said. "Snakes and poison bugs! They live in the depths of the cave."

Myka sat forward. Now, this was getting interesting! "You *think* they live in the cave," she said. "But it's all just a story."

"No, no," Clara insisted. "Don't think about going into that cave, Myka. It's much too dangerous. You need to stay home and rest. Wait a few days, and then see what happens."

"I don't want to wait!" Myka declared. She fluttered her wings, impatient. The more Clara spoke of the dangers, the more Myka wanted to explore the cave. She couldn't just sit around Bess's studio sorting mouse hairs!

"I'm going!" she announced.

"I'll take you," Bess volunteered.

"I don't need anyone to take me," Myka scoffed. "I'm not some newly arrived fairy. I don't need anyone's help."

Then she paused and spoke quietly. "Bess, I'm a scout. This is something I have to do on my own."

Myka thought hard. To get to Tammarin Gorge, she'd have to fly through the orchard, over Wough River, near Torth Mountain. She'd been there many times. Of course, that was when she had perfect eyesight.

But it shouldn't be that difficult, she

reasoned. She still had her scout's sense of direction. Not to mention her other senses, too.

First things first, she thought.

She undid the moss. At least now she could see some light and shapes.

Myka flew to the edge of Pixie Hollow. If she concentrated, this part wouldn't be hard. She knew the trees and fields and streams as well as she knew her own room. Then she reached the orchard. She took a deep breath.

"Here goes," she said.

Myka flew slowly. She strained to hear leaves rustle and birds chirp. These were all clues, telling her which way to fly. When she heard a soft rustling to her left, she flew right.

"There!" she said, missing a tree.

She heard a sound to her right and swerved left to avoid a family of robins.

Tap, tap, tap, tap. That was a woodpecker straight ahead.

ZzzzZzzzz. Mosquito to her side.

Myka sniffed. A field of sweet violets.

I'm getting closer! she thought. She was almost there. Just a few more—

Thwap! She flew into a spiderweb.

8

STICKY THREADS CLUNG to Myka's body. She was stuck! She couldn't see where to pull, or even where the spider was!

She twisted and turned. But she only got more tangled.

"Here, let me help." Bess's calm voice was close by. Myka felt the web lifting away from her shoulders . . .

her legs . . . her feet. She was free!

"Bess!" Myka hugged her friend. "What are you doing here?"

"I wanted to bring you this. For the moss!" Bess held out an acorn basket. "So I followed you."

"I'm glad you did!" Myka said. Then she added quickly, "But you know, I would have been fine."

"I know," said Bess.

"Well, now that you're here, I guess you can come, too." Myka paused. "You need to stay out of the cave, though."

With Bess leading the way, it didn't take long to find Tammarin Gorge, a deep, narrow valley. Myka heard the roar of Indigo Falls and pictured water flowing over the sheer drop.

Together Myka and Bess flew down the cliffside. Myka felt the light grow dimmer. Water thundered. A strong and steady mist filled the air.

The fairies hovered in front of the falls. Bess peered up and down, side to side. "I don't see any way in," she said.

Myka fluttered around, one ear cocked. She stopped in front of a long, flat ledge. Water rushed over its side, dividing into two fast-running streams. "I think this is the spot. It's quieter. There must be a break in the water."

Bess peered closer. "I see something!" she finally exclaimed.

"All right!" Myka nodded. "I'll be out as soon as I can."

"I'm going, too." Bess sounded as

determined as her friend. "I want to see the cave. I want to paint a picture so everyone will know what it's like."

"What about the snake? And the bugs?" Myka asked.

Bess laughed. "You don't believe that nonsense, Myka. You said so! Fairy glows extinguished? Wings magically washed free of dust? Ha! Besides, it might be helpful to have a guide. Not that you need one," she added quickly.

"Fine," Myka agreed. "But I go first."

Holding hands, Myka and Bess slipped through the waterfall curtain. Inside, they landed on dusty ground.

Sssstttttt! Their glows sputtered out. The roar of the waterfall stopped. Silence pressed in on them, as if there were

nothing and no one outside the cave. "Uh-oh," Myka said quietly.

The friends stood in total darkness. If that part of the legend was true, then maybe the other dangers were real, too. Myka flapped her wings. They were too wet to fly.

Myka felt Bess tremble. "I can't see anything!" Bess whispered.

"I can't see, either," Myka told Bess.

But she had other senses. Senses, she realized, that she'd been relying on all along. Hearing. Smell. Touch . . . and her scouting sense.

"Maybe we should leave," Bess said.

Leave? When they were so close? Myka couldn't. What would make Bess as brave as any scout?

Art! Bess just had to think about her painting, and she'd feel strong.

"I'll use my senses to describe the cave," Myka told Bess. "So you can still paint it."

Bess squeezed her hand. They stepped forward.

"The air is moving over our heads," Myka went on. "So the cave is shaped like a dome." She touched the wall. "Limestone," she declared. "Rough and chalky."

They edged along the side of the cave. "Stop!" Myka pulled on Bess's arm. "Did you hear that?"

"No," Bess squeaked.

Myka strained to listen. Straight ahead. A soft, steady hissing.

The snake!

Myka listened even more closely. The hissing was regular, constant. The snake was sleeping!

With any luck, they could sneak right by. "Stay close to me," Myka whispered to Bess. "Step when I step. We're going past the snake."

Inch by inch, they crept. Slowly, carefully. "The snake is long and fat and coiled like a rope," Myka relayed to Bess. "Its head is tucked under its tail."

Minutes stretched. It seemed to take forever. The hissing grew fainter. Then it stopped. They had passed the snake! "We're safe!" Myka told Bess.

They took another step. Suddenly, the air current shifted. "The pit!" Myka whispered. "It's on the right."

They slid forward, step after step. Bess turned to Myka. "Where—" she began. Then Bess slipped.

"Oh!" One foot slid off the edge, into the yawning pit. Myka gripped Bess's hand. Clumps of dirt and rock skittered into the chasm. Bess dangled.

The basket fell from her shoulder. Down . . . down . . . down . . . never hitting bottom.

Myka reached for Bess's other hand. Holding tightly, she leaned back and dragged her friend to safety.

Moving even more slowly now, they sidled along the cave wall. Myka stopped suddenly. She sniffed. A new smell mingled with the air, almost like wet laundry. "Do you smell that?" she asked.

"No," Bess whispered.

Then she heard the sound of tiny legs. They skittered on the stone floor.

The poison bugs! Directly ahead!

"I can tell they're not very big," said Myka. "And there are rocks all around them." Myka linked arms with Bess. "Jump when I jump," she instructed.

Myka led the way, leaping over bugs as if they were chestnut checkers pieces.

They vaulted over one last bug and landed on the cave floor.

"We're almost halfway around the cave," Myka told Bess.

She put her hand to the side. The wall felt different—not quite so powdery. And even with her fading eyesight, she saw a slight glimmer of light ahead.

"The sides are growing damp," Myka said. She and Bess shuffled forward. "We're almost there. The shimmer moss is right . . ."

Myka touched a soft, spongy spot. "Here!"

9

ONE HOUR LATER, Myka and Bess stood just inside the cave's entrance. They'd stuffed their pockets with shimmer moss. Then they'd made their way back.

They were set to dash through the waterfall curtain. They had to land on the ledge outside. If they missed . . .

Myka didn't let herself think about

it. They had no choice but to try. There was no other way.

"Ready?" asked Myka.

"Ready," said Bess.

Still holding hands, they jumped through the water. There was a moment of nothingness. Then their feet landed on stone. The ledge!

Myka and Bess moved away from the waterfall mist so that their wings could dry. It took a while, but they were finally able to lift off.

Slowly at first, then gaining speed, the fairies flew through forests, over the river and the orchard.

"No arguments," Bess told Myka when they reached Pixie Hollow. "We're going straight to the infirmary."

Hovering in front of the door a few minutes later, Myka reached for the knob. But the door swung open before she even touched it. Clara pulled her inside, hugging her tightly.

"I've been waiting! I've been so worried, I was going to get the other scouts to find you!"

"Why, Clara, I'm glad to see you, too." Then Myka laughed. "I mean, I'm glad to *hear* you. Are you ready to put the shimmer moss over my eyes?"

"Of course!" Clara exclaimed at once. "Come sit down."

With Bess watching, Clara wrapped the shimmer moss over Myka's eyes. Then she led her to a cushiony cot in the corner. "Now rest here."

Myka stretched out and yawned. Clara put a soft blanket over her. All the flying . . . the close calls . . . The bed felt so comfortable. . . . So cozy . . .

"Of course you'll stay the night," Clara said.

"What?" Myka sat up. "Can't I sleep in my own room?"

"Nurse's orders," Clara said briskly. "I'm not taking any chances," she added in a softer voice.

"I'll stay with you until you fall asleep," Bess offered.

"No, no," Myka insisted. "That would take too long. You know me. I never need much sleep. You just—zzzzz."

Myka was fast asleep.

Hours passed. When Myka woke, it was the next day, midafternoon. All around her, she heard murmurs.

"Who's there?" she said.

"You're awake!" said Bess.

"Clara? Are you here, too?" Myka asked.

"Yes," said the nursing talent.

Myka sensed other fairies in the room. "Who else? No—wait! I can tell." She smelled porcupine quills. "Trak and Sera." She heard the rustle of a long petal dress. "And Queen Clarion!"

"Right!" Trak said. "We're all here. We're all waiting to see what happens."

"Is it time to take off the moss?" asked Myka.

"Yes." Clara stepped closer to the cot. "It is." She patted Myka's hand. "Are you ready?"

"Of course!" Myka answered. But was she really? What if she opened her eyes and her vision wasn't any better? What if the shimmer moss was just ordinary moss, with no magic in it at all?

There'd be no more patrols. No more soaring through the sky listening for hawk cries. No more excitement. No more helping her friends.

Gently, Clara unwound the moss. She lifted it from Myka's eyes. "There!" she said.

For a moment, Myka kept her eyes closed. Then, little by little, she opened them.

She blinked. Once, twice. "I can see!" she cried.

Sunshine streamed brightly through the window. A metal chair gleamed. Bess's smile glowed. "I can see as well as ever!"

Myka turned to Trak. He stared at her, a questioning look in his eyes. "How

do we know for sure, Myka? You've tried to fool us before."

"Oh, Trak! I'd fly backward if I could. I shouldn't have pretended. I just didn't want to stop scouting!"

He smiled. He understood. "And now?"

"And now I can see! In fact, I see you just had a poppy puff roll."

"What?" said Trak.

Myka leaned forward and picked a crumb from under his shirt collar.

"Okay, Myka." Trak laughed. "I confess! I sneaked into the kitchen before I came here."

"So are you ready to go on patrol?" asked Myka.

10

MYKA HAD LUNCH before patrolling Pixie Hollow. She was starving! As she ate, she glanced around happily. The tearoom had never looked so lovely. Dulcie's muffins had never tasted so good. Fairy chatter had never sounded so musical.

"I'm glad you're better, Myka!" Beck called out.

"Fly with you soon!" Tink beamed. "We'll search out that coin together!"

Myka soaked up all the good feeling. She didn't want to waste time, though. She was itching to do some scouting. But she had to take care of one thing first. . . .

She darted out the nearest window and flew quickly to Bess's studio.

"I see you're done already!" she told her friend. The cave picture sat drying on an easel. There was the pit . . . and the snake . . . and the poison bugs. "It looks just like I thought!"

Next, she flew outside. It felt so good to be outdoors!

Myka waved to a butterfly herder, a dust talent, and even Iris. Then she flew to the eucalyptus tree lookout. She peered in all directions.

She saw ants carrying crumbs in a faraway field. She saw inchworms sliding up trees in a distant wood. Everything looked fine.

She raised the whistle to blow the all-clear signal. But then she stopped.

A faint sound was coming from the other side of the forest. What was it?

Myka stood at the edge of the platform. She grabbed a leaf and shaped it into a funnel to catch the sound. Holding the leaf cone to her ear, she listened.

Bzzzz. Bzzzzz.

Bees!

Slowly, the sound grew louder. It was

a whole swarm! And it was heading their way! She blew three quick shrills on the whistle. Danger! Danger! Myka dove from the tree in a burst of speed.

Racing, she darted through Pixie Hollow. She was almost to the court-yard. First she'd find the other scouts. She'd tell—

"Trak!" she cried, nearly crashing into him. "There's a swarm of bees flying toward the Home Tree!"

Below, a group of fairies overheard.

"Can we believe her?" a harvesting-talent fairy asked.

"Yes." "No." "Yes." Each fairy had a different opinion. Myka ignored them all.

"Please, Trak," she begged.

Trak flew to the upper branch of the Home Tree. He raised his binoculars and turned in a circle. "I don't see a thing," he called down. "I don't see one bee!"

"I don't see them, either!" Myka said hurriedly. "I hear them!"

She turned to Queen Clarion, who had flown to her side. "I do," Myka said quietly. "I hear them."

Trak and Queen Clarion looked at each other. They both nodded.

"Beck!" Trak called to the animal talent. "Let's work together."

Beck signaled Fawn to come, too. "We need to send the bees another way," she said. "Myka! Take us to the swarm."

Myka led them to the edge of Pixie Hollow. She pointed to the other side of the forest. A giant black and yellow cloud of bees swept closer. They were buzzing angrily.

Myka caught her breath.

Beck and Fawn stood their ground. As the bees drew nearer, they pointed to the mountains. They called out. To Myka, it sounded like ZZZZZzzzzZZZZ.

Suddenly, the entire swarm turned

around. The buzzing cloud moved farther and farther away.

"What did you say?" asked Myka.

Beck grinned. "We told them about an amazing field, chock-full of sweet-smelling flowers!"

"You're a hero!" Myka told Beck.

Beck smiled even wider. "You too, Myka."

It seemed that all of Pixie Hollow was waiting for them to return. Fairies and sparrow men clapped and cheered.

"Hooray for Myka!" Trak's voice rose above all the others.

Myka's glow flared with pride. She was the top scout once again! And after everything that had happened? She was a better one, too.